s. Do not mind large seed, it will soften in cooking. Crush half of the berries and

ut into pieces. Cook over low heat, stirring all the while until sugar is dissolved.

tle jam. **Blackberry Jam:** In a kettle add one cup of water to four cups of

d is formed when you lift spoon. Add four heaping cups of blackberries and boil for

th paraffin. If you mind the seeds, you can first sieve all or a part of the berries

Gently pick over and stem wild strawberries. Do not wash. Put one half pint straw-

ing them whole. Cover berries with four cups white sugar. Stir mixture carefully

rent burning. Remove from heat when berries have bubbled up, about fifteen minutes.

bine 1 1/4 cup water, two cups sugar, 1/8 teaspoon ground cloves, a pinch of cinnamon, a

dissolved. Bring to a boil and boil for seven minutes. Add three pints blueberries.

inue to boil the syrup for ten minutes or until thick. Return the blueberries to the

y gathered, ripe raspberries into a large jar. Mash the fruit a little with a wooden

he juice has seeped from the fruit, sieve the juice. Allow 3/4 pound of sugar for

ns and stays firm when put onto a saucer. Bottle while hot and cover with paraffin.

Sleeping Bear Press

Text copyright © 2002 Gloria Whelan
Illustration copyright © Gijsbert van Frankenhuyzen

Sleeping Bear Press
310 North Main Street
P.O. Box 20
Chelsea, MI 48118
www.sleepingbearpress.com

Printed and bound in Canada.

10 9 8 7 6 5 4 3 2 1

Library of Congress Cataloging-in-Publication Data
Whelan, Gloria.
Jam & jelly by Holly & Nellie / Gloria Whelan ; illustrator,
Gijsbert van Frankhuyzen.
p. cm.
Summary: Nellie and her mother pick berries all summer
in order to make enough money so that Nellie can get a coat
to wear to school in the winter.
ISBN 1-58536-109-7
[1. Bears—Fiction. 2. Berries—Fiction 3. Mothers and daughters—Fiction.]
I. Frankhuyzen, Gijsbert van, ill. II. Title.
III. Title: Jam and jelly by Holly and Nellie.
PZ7.W5718Jam 2002
[E]—dc21
2002012752

Written by Gloria Whelan

Illustrated by Gijsbert van Frankenhuyzen

To Brendan Whelan

—Gloria

For Robbyn, Heather, and Kelly

—Gijsbert

ILLUSTRATOR'S ACKNOWLEDGMENTS

My models for *Jam & Jelly* turned into a family project. I started off looking for a little girl and ended up with a mom and dad, too. Many thanks to Mark and Dawn Garfield for giving up several of your summer evenings to act out Gloria's wonderful story. And to Randi, a beautiful Holly, thank you for posing over and over and over again. You were very patient. It was great working with you all.

"Holly starts school this fall," Mama tells Papa. "She'll need a warm coat and boots."

We live in northern Michigan where the winter wind lays hold of you and the snow falls until everything is like a sheet of white paper.

Papa shakes his head meaning, No. "You can't expect money from carrots that grow in sand or cabbages that have to push away rocks on their way up. When the weather gets bad, Holly will have to keep to the house."

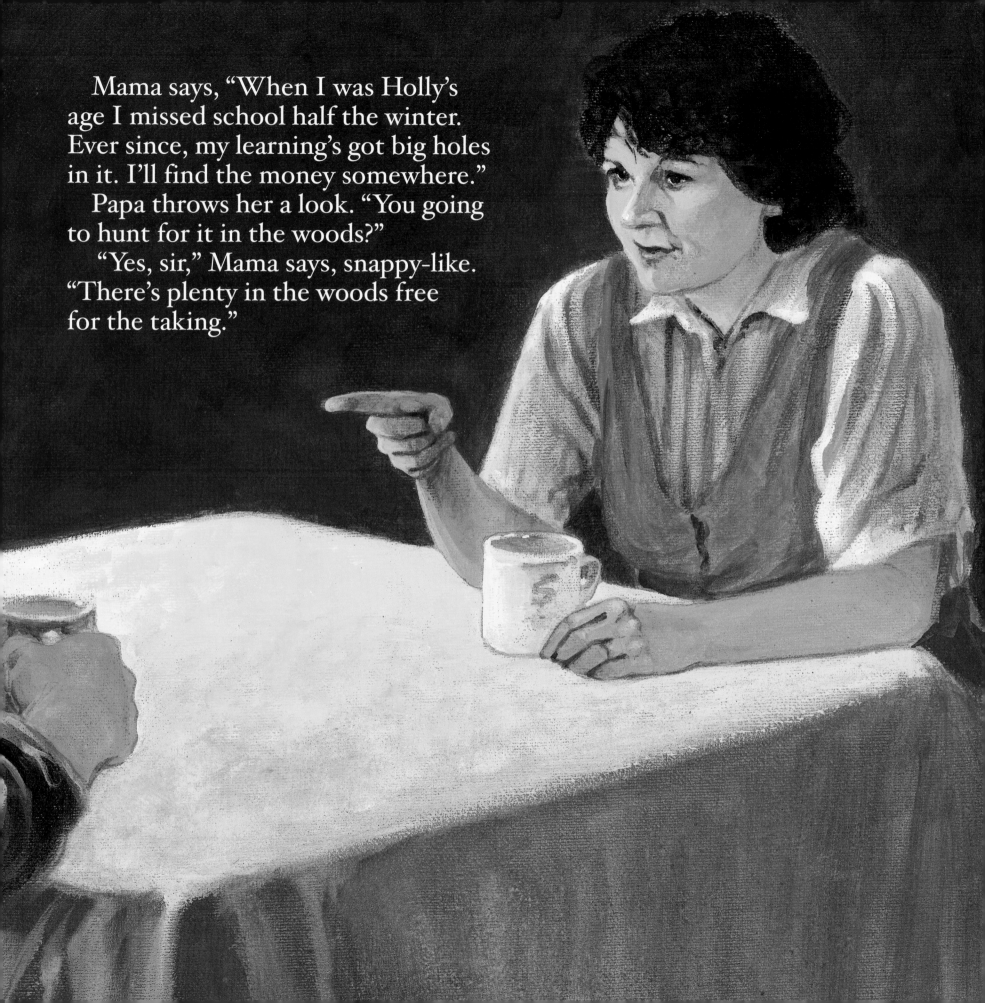

Mama says, "When I was Holly's age I missed school half the winter. Ever since, my learning's got big holes in it. I'll find the money somewhere."

Papa throws her a look. "You going to hunt for it in the woods?"

"Yes, sir," Mama says, snappy-like. "There's plenty in the woods free for the taking."

The end of June, Mama and me are
on our knees. We're pushing aside field
daisies, butter-and-eggs, and goatsbeard.
We're looking for wild strawberries.

Hunkered down under the bracken fern
I'm eye to eye with a daddy-longlegs walking
on stilts and a green beetle so shiny he looks
like he turned a light on inside himself.

The strawberries are no bigger than the nail on my little finger. It takes a long time to cover the bottom of my basket. Mama's basket is nearly full. I'm hot and my knees hurt from kneeling. Red pepper ants stick their needles into me. I say, "Can't we stop now?"

Mama tells me, "Listen to what the ovenbird says."

The bird calls, "Teacher, teacher, teacher."

I don't want holes in my learning so I keep picking.

Back home in the kitchen Mama gets the kettle boiling. I can smell strawberries all through the house. Papa and me get to eat the skimmings.

Mama's a saver. She's got a cupboard full of empty jars. Besides jelly jars there's mayonnaise jars and peanut butter jars and mustard jars. Soon the empty jars are full and there's a whole row of strawberry jam. You can see the tiny berries like red fish swimming in a red sea.

Mama and I hurry down by the river
to get the Juneberries before the birds
finish them off. The waxwings are there
with their feathery cowlicks and black
masks. The grosbeaks are there with
their red bibs and sweet songs. I pick
from the low branches. Mama picks
from the middle. The birds get the top.

I can't keep my eyes off the busy river. Trout swim by, fast as a wink. A blue heron fishes for frogs. A duck paddles by, pulling five ducklings on a string behind her.

I'm so hot I feel like melted butter. Mama and I take off our
shoes and socks. When we put our feet in the river we yelp
with the cold. Mama says we got work to do and can't sit long.

A dragonfly with windowpane wings lights on my arm.
When a snapping turtle swims near our toes we hurry out.

Raspberries grow in the open. The July sun is noon hot but we've got on straw hats so it can't get to us. The Queen Anne's lace has put up its white umbrellas. Each milkweed flower has an orange butterfly dangling like an earring.

More raspberries go into my mouth than go into my basket. Near one of the bushes is a woodchuck hole. The woodchuck is lucky, living in the middle of a raspberry patch. I find the burrow's back door. If a fox sticks his nose in the front, the woodchuck can hurry out the back.

Mama whistles while she's picking. She can whistle birdsongs.
A warbler pipes its song from the top of an oak tree. Mama
answers back. So does the warbler. Back and forth the songs go.
I ask Mama what the warbler is saying.
    "Summer afternoon,
       summer afternoon,
         summer afternoon."

Mama keeps some raspberries from the kettle. For dessert we have raspberry pie. I have two pieces. Papa has three. "I got a surprise for you," he tells me and Mama, but he won't say what it is. "It'll be ready when you're ready," he says.

The blueberries grow on a hill. It's the hottest July ever, so we pick in the evening cool. The hillside is covered with springy moss. It's like kneeling on a pillow.

The berries are different colors. Some are green like the moss, some are pink as roses, some are lavender like lilacs. None of those berries are done yet. Mama says, "Just pick the berries that are blue."

There are oak and pine seedlings pushing up through the moss. It wasn't a farmer who planted them. The chipmunks buried the acorns and the squirrels buried the pine seeds. The seedlings are small now but Mama says when they start growing they'll catch me up.

The moss is moving! Only it's not the moss. It's a green snake, thin as a pencil. We take off in different directions.

Going home it's nearly dark.
Everything looks softer. There
are moon shadows. I step on the
black stripes of tree trunks.

A whippoorwill says its name.

In bed I hear an owl ask the same question over and over. "Who? Who? Who?" I dream I open the door to the schoolhouse and inside it's full up with berries.

Blackberries come last. It's nearly fall. The maple trees are starting to put out their red flags. There's no more birdsong in the woods. Last night Papa had to cover his tomatoes with newspaper to keep out the frost.

The blackberries fight me off with their brambly thorns. They scratch and claw at me and snag my hair. I say, "Maybe it wouldn't be so bad missing some school days." Mama says, "Holly, they tell you stories in school. The day you miss might be the best story of all."

But I don't know how all the berries will turn into a coat and boots.

We pick all week and there are still blackberries left on the bushes. Mama makes blackberry jam and jelly and pie and muffins. You can't turn around in the house without running into a blackberry.

One night coming home we see sleepy bumblebees hugging the goldenrod flowers. The chilly bees are waiting for the morning sun to warm them up.

At last it's time for Papa's surprise. He's built a stand for us and put it right next to the road. It has shelves to hold Mama's jars. He's painted a sign that says: Jam & Jelly by Holly & Nellie. Holly, that's my name and it's right out there for anyone to see. We fill up the shelves. With the sun shining on them the rows of purple and red and blue jars look like our church window.

Mama has to bake bread. She says, "You mind the stand for me, Holly."

It's a long time before a car stops. "How much?"
the driver asks. "Twenty-five cents a jar," I say.
The man drives off, fast, leaving
me and the jars all dusty.

Another car comes by.
A lady winds down her window.
"How much?" she asks.
    "Twenty-five cents a jar,"
I say. I hold my breath.
    "I'll take one raspberry
and one blueberry," she says.

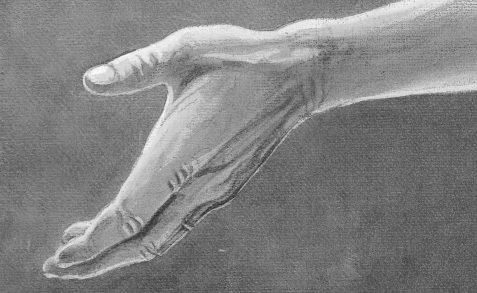

She gives me a quarter, a dime, two nickels and
five pennies. I put them in Mama's last empty jar.

By the time school starts the shelves
are empty and the jar is full.

The October wind blows the leaves off the trees. In November the rain puddles freeze over. In December our roof has a fringe of icicles. Waiting for the school bus, the wind and the snow swirl around me until I nearly disappear. Papa calls out to be sure I'm still there. All winter my coat keeps out the wind. My boots keep out the snow.

What keeps me warmest of all is remembering the smell of the strawberries, the busy river, the raspberry pie, the colors of blueberries, sleepy bumblebees, and Papa's surprise.

GLORIA WHELAN

Gloria Whelan is a poet and the award-winning author of many books including *Homeless Bird*, for which she received the National Book Award. She lives with her husband, Joe, in the woods of northern Michigan.

GIJSBERT VAN FRANKENHUYZEN

Gijsbert was born in the Netherlands. Always drawing as a young boy, his father encouraged Gijsbert to make art his career. After high school, he attended and graduated from the Royal Academy of Arts in Arnhem. He immigrated to America in 1976 and worked as Art Director for the Michigan *Natural Resources Magazine* for 17 years. Gijsbert now paints full-time and loves the freedom of painting whatever he wants.

Jam & Jelly by Holly & Nellie is his 11th children's book with Sleeping Bear Press. His other titles include *The Legend of Sleeping Bear, Adopted by an Owl,* and most recently *Mercedes and the Chocolate Pilot.*

Gijsbert and his family live in Bath, Michigan, where they share their 40-acre farm with sheep, horses, dogs, cats, turkeys, rabbits, chickens, and pigeons. They also provide a temporary home for many orphaned and injured wildlife. The farm, the land, and the animals make great subjects for the artist to paint.

Juneberry Jam: Wash four cups juneberries being sure to remove small add the remaining whole berries. Combine with three cups of sugar. Add two app Simmer over low heat, stirring, until a spoonful dropped onto a plate remains firm. sugar and bring to a rolling boil. Boil about two or three minutes until a slight th twelve minutes. Let stand overnight in enamel pan. Put in sterilized jars and cove making sure you have four cups of sieved berries. **Wild Strawberry Jar** berries into iron pot and crush. Add the remaining pint and a half of strawberries, over low heat until juice appears. Raise heat to medium and do not stir other than to Cool jam and bottle. **Spiced Blueberry Conserve:** In a large kettle pinch of nutmeg and 1 $^{1/2}$ cups red wine vinegar. Stir over medium heat until the sug Bring to boil again and boil for two minutes. Remove the blueberries to a bowl and syrup and boil for four minutes. Bottle while hot. **Raspberry Jelly:** Put fr spoon. Cover the jar and place it in a kettle of boiling water. In about an hour w every pint of juice. Boil the sugar and the juice over a low fire until the jelly th